Famous Legends

The Legend of King Arthur

By Shalini Saxena

 Gareth Stevens
PUBLISHING

Please visit our website, www.garethstevens.com. For a free color catalog of all our high-quality books, call toll free 1-800-542-2595 or fax 1-877-542-2596.

Library of Congress Cataloging-in-Publication Data

Saxena, Shalini.
The legend of King Arthur / by Shalini Saxena.
p. cm. — (Famous legends)
Includes index.
ISBN 978-1-4824-2736-3 (pbk.)
ISBN 978-1-4824-2737-0 (6 pack)
ISBN 978-1-4824-2738-7 (library binding)
1. Arthur, — King — Juvenile literature. 2. Britons — Kings and rulers — Juvenile literature. 3. Great Britain — History — To 1066 — Juvenile literature. I. Saxena, Shalini, 1982-. II. Title.
DA152.5.A7 S29 2016
942.01'4—d23

First Edition

Published in 2016 by
Gareth Stevens Publishing
111 East 14th Street, Suite 349
New York, NY 10003

Copyright © 2016 Gareth Stevens Publishing

Designer: Laura Bowen
Editor: Therese Shea

Photo credits: Cover, pp. 1, 15, 19, 21 DEA Picture Library/De Agnosti Picture Library/Getty Images; cover, p. 1 (ribbon) barbaliss/Shutterstock.com; cover, p. 1 (leather) Pink Pueblo/Shutterstock.com; cover, pp. 1–32 (sign) Sarawut Padungkwan/Shutterstock.com; cover, pp. 1–32 (vines) vitasunny/Shutterstock.com; cover, pp. 1–32 (parchment) TyBy/Shutterstock.com; cover, pp. 1–32 (background) HorenkO/Shutterstock.com; pp. 5, 9, 17 N.C. Wyeth/ Wikimedia Commons; p. 7 Matthew Paris/Wikimedia Commons; p. 11 GraphicaArtis/Hulton Archive/Getty Images; p. 13 Charles Ernest Butler/Wikimedia Commons; p. 23 Hulton Archive/Getty Images; p. 25 Mansell/ The LIFE Picture Collection/Getty Images; p. 27 Print Collector/Hulton Archive/Getty Images; p. 29 (main) Ethan Myerson/E+/Getty Images; p. 29 (inset) Daderot/Wikimedia Commons.

Printed in the United States of America

CPSIA compliance information: Batch #CS15GS: For further information contact Gareth Stevens, New York, New York at 1-800-542-2595.

Contents

Words in the glossary appear in **bold** type the first time they are used in the text.

Myth or Reality?

In a land of castles, **warriors**, and magic, one young boy grew to become a great hero and king. With a group of noble knights, he went on quests filled with adventure. He fought in many important battles and brought peace to ancient Britain. This is the **legend** of King Arthur.

There are different accounts of this story, but most include these basic elements. It might sound like a fairy tale, but many believe that some parts of the legend are true!

The Inside Story

According to history, the real Arthur probably lived in the fifth or sixth century. However, many stories about him take place much later—between the 12th and 15th centuries.

According to legend, King Arthur was one of the most beloved kings of Britain.

5

A King Is Born

A long time ago, Britain was a land always at war. Many different groups fought each other to control it. During this **turmoil**, a man called Uther (OO-thur) Pendragon became high king of Britain.

One day, Uther's wife Igraine (ee-GRAYN) gave birth to a son. Before the child was born, Uther had promised to give him to his advisor, the magician Merlin. Merlin knew the baby, Arthur, would grow to be a great man someday if he was raised correctly. And so, baby Arthur was taken away.

The Inside Story

The word "Pendragon" is actually a title, not a name. It means "head dragon."

Uther Pendragon was a powerful warrior and strong leader. He was a Briton who fought groups like the Irish, Saxons from Germany, and Picts from Scotland.

Mastering Body and Mind

Merlin took Arthur to the home of Sir Ector, a knight. Ector already had a son named Kay, but he took Arthur in and raised both boys. Nobody knew that Arthur was the king's son.

As the boys grew older, Ector taught Kay and Arthur how to fight well and with honor. These were two features of a good knight. Around this time, Merlin began to teach Arthur different subjects. He also taught him knowledge was better than strength. He wanted him to be a just man and ruler.

The Inside Story

The legend of Arthur has many elements of Celtic myths, which are stories from Wales, Ireland, and Scotland. Merlin is said to be like characters from Celtic stories.

Ector showed Arthur how to use his strength. Merlin showed him how to use his mind. Merlin knew that if Arthur had both these tools, he could be a great leader.

9

The Sword in the Stone

Uther died, and for long after, Britain had no king. In order to become king, someone had to pull a magic sword from a stone in London. For years, many tried, but all failed. The sword in the stone was forgotten for a time.

When Arthur was 15, he went to London with Ector and Kay, so Kay could fight in a **tournament**. Arthur acted as Kay's **squire**. However, he forgot Kay's sword! Arthur went to look for one. He came upon the sword in the stone and pulled it out easily.

The Inside Story

Knights were strong warriors. They fought in tournaments against each other to show their skill and win prizes.

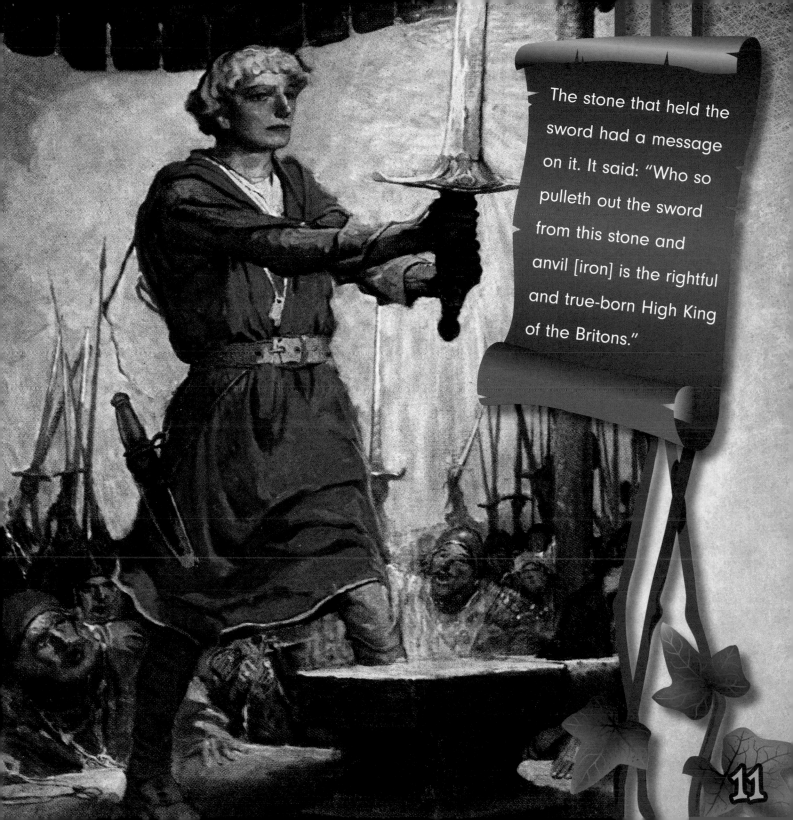

The stone that held the sword had a message on it. It said: "Who so pulleth out the sword from this stone and anvil [iron] is the rightful and true-born High King of the Britons."

11

A New King Is Crowned

Arthur didn't know that there was anything special about the sword. But Kay knew it was unusual. He asked Arthur where it was from. Kay and Ector were amazed by his answer.

They all returned to the stone. Arthur put the sword back into it. Kay and others tried to pull it out, but they failed. However, Arthur took the sword out of the stone again and again. Everyone realized Arthur was the real **heir** to the throne. He was crowned king of Britain.

The Inside Story

Some legends say that the sword from the stone was called Galatine or Sequence.

Though some thought such a young and weak boy couldn't possibly be the true king, Arthur would prove to be a wise, fair, and brave ruler.

13

The Road to Camelot

Arthur had much to do after being crowned. He needed to set up his court. He had to find knights and advisors he could trust. Merlin arrived to help him get his court in order. He advised Arthur to rule his kingdom from the court of Camelot.

Soon after being crowned, Arthur held a royal dinner, but some of the invited nobles decided to declare war on the young ruler instead. They didn't think Arthur was fit to be king. Arthur **defeated** his enemies, gaining the respect of many.

The Inside Story

Camelot's location is a mystery. Some say it was in Wales. Others say that it was in one of several possible places in England.

During Arthur's rule, Camelot was known as a great kingdom where many found peace and happiness.

15

The Rise of Excalibur

Soon after he was crowned, the sword Arthur had drawn from the stone broke. He needed a new sword to **defend** himself in battle. Merlin took Arthur to the edge of a lake. After a few moments, a woman's arm appeared holding a beautiful sword. Arthur took the sword, and the woman's arm disappeared.

Merlin explained the woman was the Lady of the Lake. She was very powerful, and so was her gift. The sword was called Excalibur. It would help Arthur win many battles.

The Inside Story

Most stories agree that Arthur had two different swords.

The word "Excalibur" is said to mean "cut steel." The sword's power is as legendary as King Arthur himself.

The Knights of the Round Table

Arthur fell in love with a beautiful noblewoman named Guinevere. They were married, and she became queen of Camelot. Guinevere's father gave the couple a large round table as a wedding present.

Arthur used the table for his Order of the Round Table. This group was made up of the most honorable and loyal, or faithful, knights in Britain. Ector and Kay were among them. Another famous knight was Lancelot. The Knights of the Round Table performed many brave and good deeds.

The Inside Story

Arthur's Round Table could seat 150 people. Since there was no head, everyone who sat at it was considered equal in greatness.

The Knights of the Round Table helped Arthur in battles and quests. There are many stories about their adventures.

A Noble Quest

One night, Arthur and his knights had a **vision** of a golden cup. It was the Holy Grail, the cup Jesus was said to have used at the Last Supper. Arthur sent his knights to find it. The Grail's guardian was called the Fisher King. Only he knew who was worthy enough—the most noble and pure—to take the cup.

Arthur's knights faced magical beasts, evil knights, and more, but failed to bring the Grail to Camelot. Finally, Lancelot's son Galahad proved himself worthy of the Grail.

The Inside Story

Merlin had told Arthur that the Holy Grail could protect Britain.

In the vision, Arthur and his knights saw the golden cup floating over the table where they feasted. It disappeared, but they knew it was the Holy Grail.

21

Betrayal

Even though Sir Galahad reached the Grail, he didn't bring it back to King Arthur. Once he touched it, both he and the Grail disappeared.

Arthur began to face great problems. Many of his knights were gone or dead because of the quest to find the Grail. Even worse, people he trusted most **betrayed** him. Lancelot, the king's close friend, and Queen Guinevere had fallen in love. When Arthur found out about this, he was angry. He almost killed Guinevere, but Lancelot saved her. They ran away together.

The Inside Story

After he touched the Grail, Galahad became its new guard. He and the Grail moved to a secret place.

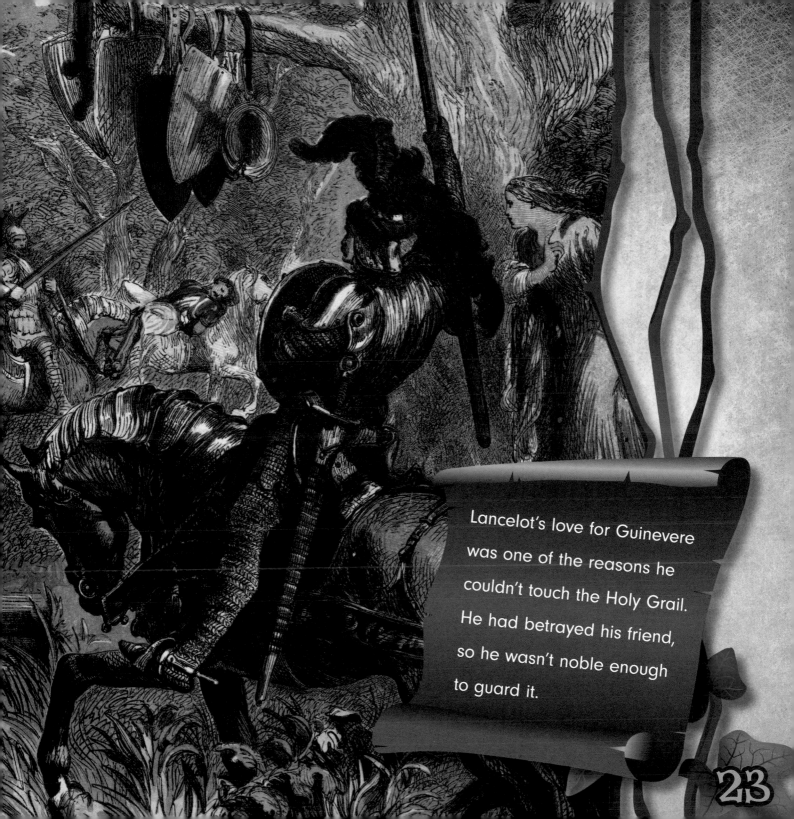

Lancelot's love for Guinevere was one of the reasons he couldn't touch the Holy Grail. He had betrayed his friend, so he wasn't noble enough to guard it.

The Fall of King Arthur

Arthur left Camelot to go to battle against Lancelot.

While he was gone, his nephew Mordred was in charge.

Mordred was next in line for the throne, but he was greedy.

He didn't want to wait, so he named himself king.

Arthur gave up his fight against Lancelot to return home.
A terrible battle between Mordred's army and Arthur's knights
followed. Arthur faced Mordred alone. He put a **spear**
through Mordred, killing him. But Mordred had hit Arthur
on the head before he died, seriously
wounding the king.

The battle between Arthur's and Mordred's forces is called the Battle of Camlann. Only one person survived.

25

The Once and Future King

Bedivere, a loyal knight of Camelot, was the only one to survive the bloody battle. The dying Arthur asked Bedivere to throw Excalibur back into the lake it came from. Bedivere did as Arthur asked. Before the sword hit the water, the Lady of the Lake reached up and caught it.

This meant Arthur could die in peace. A boat took his body to the magical Isle of Avalon. After, Bedivere heard Arthur's voice whisper that when Britain needed him again, he would return.

A legend says that the Lady of the Lake healed Arthur at Avalon.

27

Keeping Arthur's Legacy Alive

If you look in a history book about England, you won't see a king named Arthur or find Camelot on a map. But many, many writers helped bring Arthur's legend to life. They took some elements from Celtic myths and some from history.

Thomas Malory completed one of the most famous **versions** of the story around 1470. Other famous Arthurian authors are Geoffrey of Monmouth and Alfred, Lord Tennyson. These and other writers made Arthur a beloved **symbol** of honor and bravery in England and around the world.

The Inside Story

There are more legends about Arthur's knights, Merlin the magician, and other characters, such as the magical Morgan le Fay. Find these stories at your local library.

Even though we may never know if Arthur really existed, people continue to look for signs of the king's return.

Glossary

betray: to hurt someone who trusts you by doing something wrong

defeat: to win a battle or contest against someone

defend: to fight to protect against danger

heir: a person who will receive another person's property, rights, or title after their death

legend: a story that has been passed down for many, many years that's unlikely to be true

spear: a weapon with a long shaft and sharp head or blade

squire: a young man in the Middle Ages who helped a knight

symbol: someone or something that stands for an idea or ideas

tournament: a series of contests testing the skills of knights

turmoil: a state of confusion or disorder

version: a story that is different in some way from another person's story of the same events

vision: an image dreamt or seen as part of a religious or supernatural experience

warrior: a person who fights in battles and is known for having courage and skill

For More Information

Books

Lee, Tony. *Excalibur: The Legend of King Arthur*. Somerville, MA: Candlewick Press, 2011.

Limke, Jeff. *King Arthur: Excalibur Unsheathed: An English Legend*. Minneapolis, MN: Graphic Universe, 2007.

Websites

King Arthur & the Knights of the Round Table
www.kingarthursknights.com
Find out more about the Knights of the Round Table and check out some history related to King Arthur.

King Arthur for Kids
files.nyu.edu/amd402/public/arthur/kids.html
Read about the legend of King Arthur and other connected characters.

King Arthur: The History, the Legend, the King
www.britannia.com/history/h12.html
Learn about King Arthur's importance in Britain and the places you can visit that might have clues about Arthur's life.

Index